Goodnight, Me

For Jessica, Felix, Sophie, Anouk Bibi, and Jasper

Text copyright © 2005 by Andrew Daddo
Illustrations copyright © 2005 by Emma Quay

Art created with pencil, acrylic paints, and watercolors
Typeset in Linex Sweet

First published in Australia in 2005 by Hachette Livre Australia Pty Ltd.
This edition is published by arrangement with Hachette Livre Australia Pty Ltd.
Published in the United States in 2007 by Bloomsbury U.S.A. Children's Books
175 Fifth Avenue, New York, NY 10010
Distributed to the trade by Holtzbrinck Publishers

Library of Congress Cataloging–in–Publication Data
Goodnight, me / by Andrew Daddo ; illustrations by Emma Quay. – 1st U.S. ed.
p.   cm.
Summary: A baby orangutan says goodnight to each and every part of himself until sleep finally comes.
ISBN–13: 978–1–59990–153–4 • ISBN–10: 1–59990–153–6
[1. Orangutan–Fiction. 2. Animals–Infancy–Fiction. 3. Bedtime–Fiction.] I. Quay, Emma, ill. II. Title.
PZ7.D1274Go 2007   [E]–dc22   2007002613

First U.S. Edition 2007
Printed in Singapore
1 3 5 7 9 10 8 6 4 2

All papers used by Bloomsbury U.S.A. are natural, recyclable products made from wood grown in well–managed
forests. The manufacturing processes conform to the environmental regulations of the country of origin.

Goodnight, Me

ANDREW DADDO • **ILLUSTRATIONS BY EMMA QUAY**

BLOOMSBURY
CHILDREN'S
BOOKS

Goodnight, feet.

Thanks for running me around today.

Thanks for holding
my legs together, knees.

Legs, get some rest.

We've got a lot of jumping to do tomorrow.

I don't want to hear a rumble out of you till morning, tummy.

Enough wriggling, bottom.

It's time to be still.

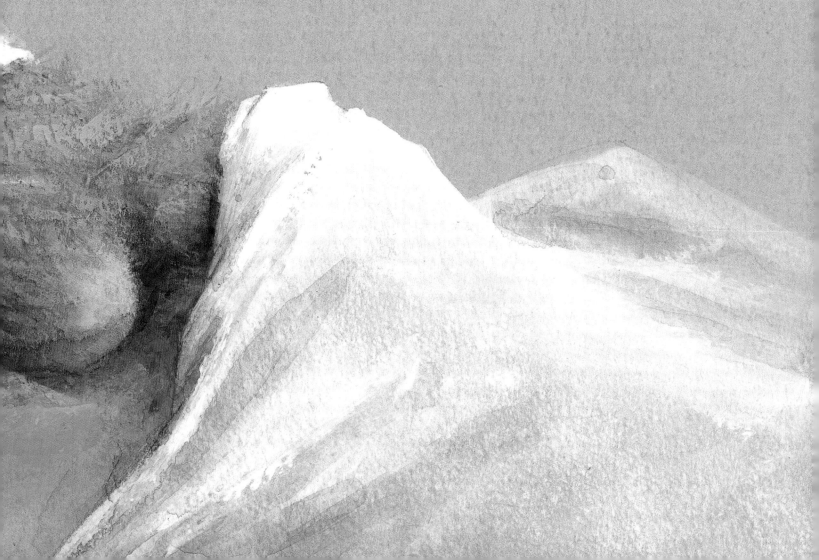

Keep breathing, chest.

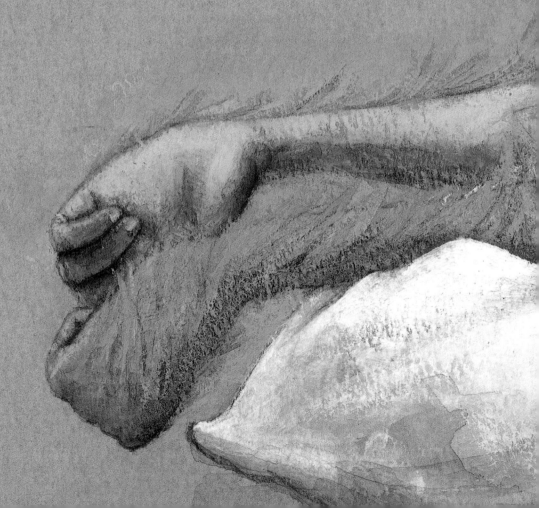

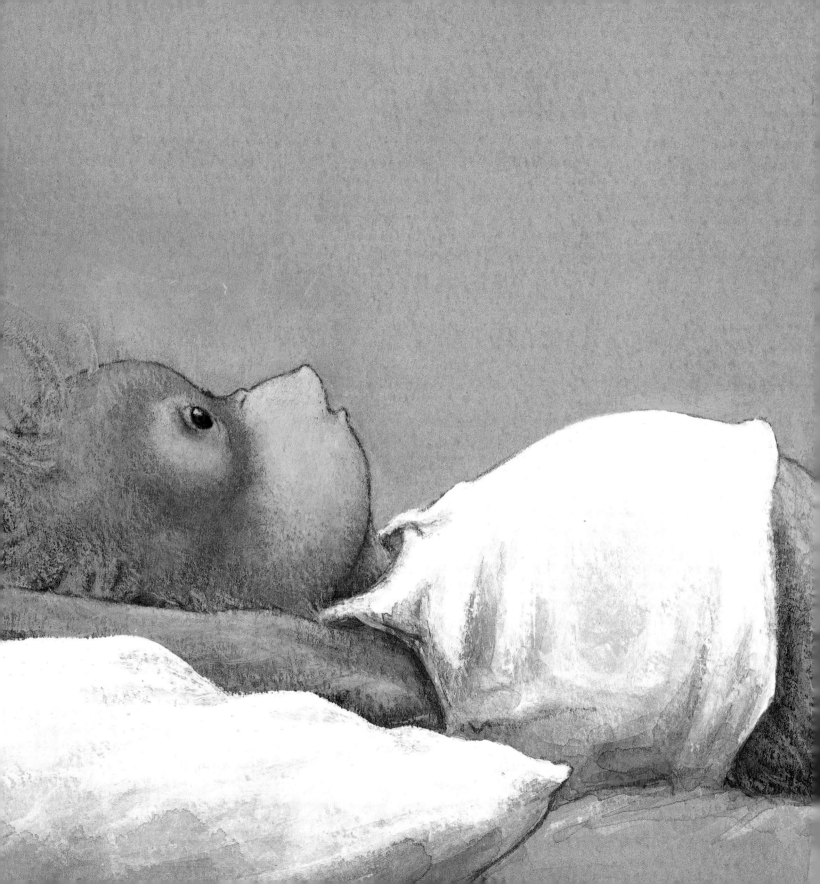

You can let go now, hands.
We're all going to sleep.

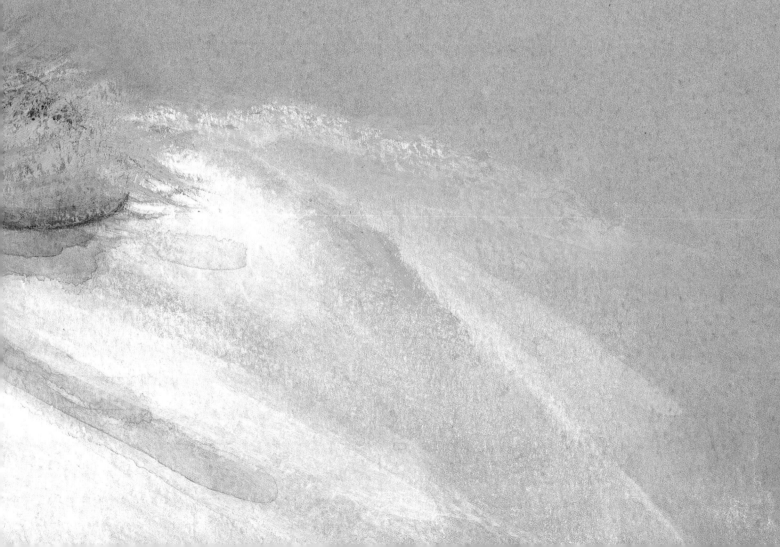

No need to hang on any longer, arms.

Is *anybody* in my body still awake?

Neck, could you please lay my head
on that pillow?
That's it. You can go to sleep now, too.

It's your turn, head.

Close those ears.

Bless you, nose!

Can you smell the sleep?

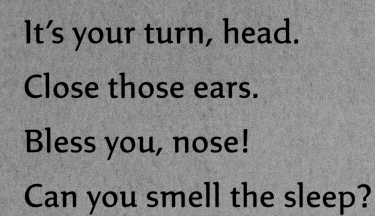

Shhh, mouth, no more questions.

Just say goodnight.

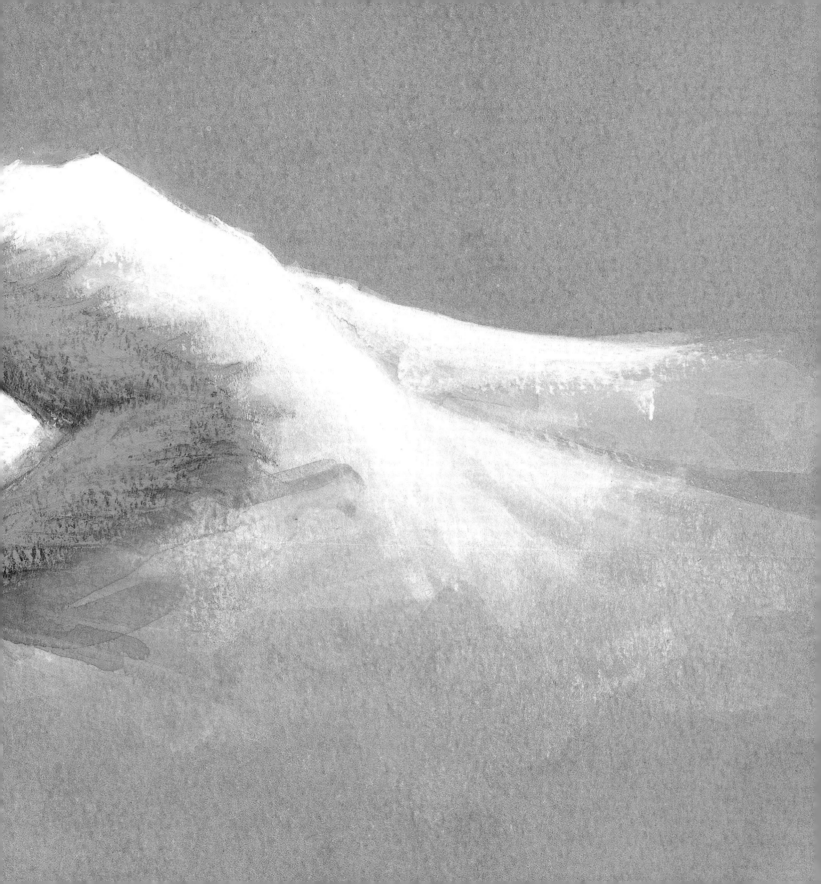

Time to close, eyes.

Can you see any dreams yet?

Goodnight, you.

I know you're still there.

I can feel you, even though
most of me is asleep.

Goodnight, me.

See you in the morning.